A Rebel's Persuasion

A Small Town Erotic Romance

Aedan Sayla

Origins of Love Company

Publisher

A Rebel's Persuasion / Aedan Sayla

Aedan Sayla

The Book List
(List last edited - 1/13/2023)

The Warriors of Mora Series

Book 1: *Submission of a Lady*
Book 2: *Warrioress Taming*
Book 3: *A Claimed Queen*
Book 4: *Possessing all of a Lady, Coming Soon*
Book 5: *The Unexpected Pleasure of a Slave, Coming Soon*

Apocalypto Series

Book 1: *A Drive to be Remembered*
Book 2: *Peril without Mercy*
Book 3: *The Will to Thrive, Coming Soon*

The Agents Series

Book 1: *Agent in Training*
Book 2: *Finding an Agent, Coming Soon*

Escaping Babylon Series

Book 1: *Foreign Princess, Coming Soon*
Book 2: *Queen in Hiding, Coming Soon*

The Badlands Series

Book 1: *The Baron Killer, Coming Soon*
Book 2: *The Cold Killers, Coming Soon*

American Apocalypse Series

Book 1: *City - Prison Land, Coming Soon*
Book 2: *Forest - Freedom Land, Coming Soon*

Standalone Books

Book: *The Huntsman*
Book: *Man on Fire*
Book: *A Russian Rose*
Book: *Tomorrow's Woman*
Book: *A Lady's Worth*
Book: *Charity's Gunman*
Book: *A Rebel's Persuasion*
Book: *Book Mate*
Book: *Brides of War*
Book: *Broken but Undefeated*
Book: *Cave Man*
Book: *Surrender's Passion*
Book: *The Forbidden Zone*
Book: *The Slave Princess, Coming Soon*
Book: *Lost, Coming Soon*
Book: *The Last Incan, Coming Soon*
Book: *His - Beauty in the Dark, Coming Soon*

Dedicated – To all the men and women, who fell in love   with each other because they found the right person to be their mate regardless of whatever their skin color was on the outside.

Content Warning

Dear reader, if per chance you did not see otherwise – this is a work of erotic fiction. The erotic content is quite vividly portrayed.

All primary sexual relations that take place are of a heterosexual standard and the age of the characters involved is 18+.

There are several scenes of 'action' violence. Racial issues are also featured within the storyline.

The appropriate reading age is 18+.

CONTENTS

The Day after Tomorrow

Graduation Day

Mandy tossed her cap into the air. She'd done it!

She had done something no one else in her family had ever achieved.

She'd completed a journey of learning and now had the benefit of looking forward to a career - a career as a cop.

Hugging her friends that had come to celebrate today with her, she went about making the most of this day that she had gone through so much hell to reach.

Simply put this day couldn't get any better.

~~~~~~~~~~

The Next Day

Staring at the sheet of paper in her hands Mandy numbly read the words over again.

Glancing up she said in a low voice, "I don't understand, Sir. I applied for the Charleston area. I don't even know where this place is!"

"In the back of nowhere is where it is. Mandy all the spots in urban areas were taken. This is all that's left. My suggestion is to make do with it and after six months reapply for relocation elsewhere in the
~~~~~~~~~~

state. By then you'll have built up experience and be better able to compete against other lesser qualified applicants."

Mandy heard his words, but all that really came through to her was that the proverbial white man culture that she was cursed to live in - had done it to her again.

Feeling the need to cry and scream at the same time, Mandy forced her full lips to remain firmly pressed together, even as she ground her teeth behind them in an effort to bite back all the things that she wanted to say.

She had been the second highest score in the class so why was she at the bottom of the list in terms of preferential placement?

Enforcing hard won civility she said, "Yes, Sir.", and left the room.

Stalking through the police academy building she got outside and breathed in deeply.

Finding a secluded place she pulled out her phone and looked up where in the heck Smithville, West Virginia, was located.

It came up and in consternation Mandy viewed over the available data.

Smithville was north - way up north. There was simply no way she would be able to commute there and back!

She would have to relocate.

"Oh God, what have you done to me?" She whispered.

Her eyes scanned down over the census data.

'Town population 738 as of 2008. - 89% of residents meet or below the poverty level. - Population demographics 97% white, 3% other.'

Angry tears streaked down Mandy's face.

Shaking her head, she said, "They're going to eat me alive! Why would you do this to me God?"

Wiping her tears away, Mandy did her best to fight for control of her face, but making her way to her car she felt like she had been a miserable failure at it, as so many people had stopped to watch her walk by with looks of pity in their eyes.

How was she going to make it six months in a place like Smithville where redneck was everyone's middle name?

~~~~~~~~~

Two Weeks Later

Not one of her expectations about Smithville had been off. It was as she had imagined it to be down to a, '*t*'.

It was rundown and filled full of people of the wrong color - the same color that had enslaved her kind once upon a time.

She had no use for white people, even as many of them seemed to have no use for her.

Ever since she had arrived she had felt like she was the starring member of a freak show, or better yet a game of pin the tail on the donkey, only she was the donkey.

Some people had been nice and to them she forced herself to be nice in return, but every day was a strain on her simply to continue existing and not just up and quit her job.

The other impulse she constantly warred with was the inclination to pull her gun free and start shooting the men who openly gawked at her as she went about town.

Scum was what they were. Scum and some of the women weren't much better.

Closing the door of the rundown apartment she had rented, because it was the only thing available in town, she leaned back against it for a long moment.

Truly the strain of this out of the way place, the color white, along with rebel flags and memorabilia flying everywhere had her wanting to vomit and curl up in a ball and cry.

She couldn't do that though.

No, she couldn't. She wasn't a quitter.

This was just a test.
~~~~~~~~~

She had no idea why God would be so cruel to her, but surely He had a reason.

It had better be a good reason!

CHAPTER TWO

The Unexpected

I eased my truck into park and started to get out.

The diner had just opened and I was hungry as could be for something that I hadn't cooked for myself, but at the moment I found myself distracted by an uncommon sight - a black girl, a very hot looking black girl at that.

No one else was on the street yet and she was walking away from me.

My eyes took in the uniform and the gun on her hip. She was a cop!

My - my, how the times were changing.

Suddenly she stopped walking and did something beautiful.

She bent over to pet a stray cat that had come up to her.

I knew what infatuation was and yet as my gaze took in the perfect way her ass curved out her tight trousers I acknowledged the reality that this was no normal infatuation that I was beginning to feel for this stranger.

I liked to appreciate the beauty of women as much as the next man, but it had been a long time since I had felt the need to claim one and make her mine.

Idly, my hand pulled at the front of my pants to make room for my expanding cock that was trying its best to bust its way out.

Did this girl not realize what a sight she was?

Opening the truck door I got out all the while continuing to appreciate the full toned thighs that ran down from a rear and a pair of hips meant to be taken a hold of firmly by a man's hands.

My hands.

I could only see part of her face, but what I could see was beautiful.

Her full lips were parted in a smile that showed teeth that gleamed white against the ebony darkness of her skin, even as the cat leaned into the caress of her fingers under its chin.

I let the door of the truck slam shut.

She jumped at the sound and the cat skittered away.

Straightening quickly she whirled around and I didn't miss the way her hand wandered to her gun or the haunted look that came to her eyes. Jumpy to be sure and in this town I didn't much blame her.

She took me in and immediately I could see that she disliked everything about me.

Shucks!

Smiling, I tipped my hat with a finger and called out, "Good morning to ya officer of the law. I haven't seen you before, but may I say I don't think the street of this town has ever been so becoming as it is now by being graced by your beautiful presence."

Her eyes blinked and she did a double take of me.

I watched her eyes take in the front of my pants and I let my smile grow brighter.

The look she gave me then was one of pure hate.

It seemed she was a girl with a bitter past.

That was okay. Hate I could work with, indifference...... well that was pretty much relationship death from the get-go.

"You have a pleasant day now and thanks for making mine one as well." I tipped my hat once more to her and shocked by my boldness she watched me go into the diner.

It was actually hard to walk away from her. I could stare at that woman for hours.

Her rear had been perfect, but the hourglass silhouette of her capped off with a pair of large breasts was in a word, sublime. The girl was a fertility princess on steroids and the urge to go back out on the street and stare was a real thing to be contended with.

Finding a seat in the diner I sat down. Ma Brown came to the table with a gleam in her eye.

Looking up I greeted her warmly and she responded by saying, "You should be ashamed of yourself. The girl's already half scared to death."

"Yeah, I noticed that, but I believe in being honest."

"I know, that's one of the things I've always liked about you, rebel at heart that you are."

I smiled and ordered my breakfast.

Before she left the table I asked, "You wouldn't happen to know her name would you?"

Ma Brown smiled, "Mandy. Mandy Jackson. I take it Smithville is going to be seeing a lot more of you than usual?"

To that I only smiled and in my smile was my answer.

~~~~~~~~~~

Mandy's Perspective

What a total and complete jerk!

Mandy's face flamed anew as she remembered the man from this morning.

Yes, she'd had her share of men tell her in no uncertain words or actions how attractive they felt her to be, but she had never quite experienced the guttural raw need of a man wanting to mate a woman as she'd seen in the stranger's eyes as he had looked at her this morning.

The worst of it was how confident he had seemed of that very eventuality happening.

As white men went he was very intimidating. He was of a larger stature than herself, and while she felt she could hold her own against
~~~~~~~~~~

the majority of the men in this town, who seemed to be undersized as a whole, it would not be the same with him.

He was big, but more than that his body had an easy well-developed confidence about it that said he'd been in fights before and had the expectation of winning every fight he got into.

He was a man accustomed to overcoming new challenges and right now it seemed that she represented such a challenge, else why would he have been so nice.

She was in no doubt as to what he wanted.

Despite whatever racial views he may hold, to him, she was simply a female and he wanted her, as far as positives went in concern to the jerk that was at least something.

In fact, that was where all positivity stopped though.

Still, he was different from the majority of men in town, who though attracted to her, all seemed to be ashamed of themselves for wanting a black girl.

Those men she simply wanted to kick in the nuts as it was clear as to what low degree they held people of her color. The man from this morning; however, she'd rather handcuff him to a fast-moving train so he would never return to haunt her.

Paperwork done, she rose up from behind her desk and closed down the office. Next to the sheriff and one other deputy and a part-time secretary, she was the only other occupant of the local police force.

The secretary was nice, as was the other deputy, but then he wasn't local. The sheriff was local and in a way that said everything that needed to be said about him.

He was one of the men that she would like to kick harder in the nuts than most.

Making her way outside she headed for her cruiser in the parking lot.

She always felt better when she was in her car. Maybe it was the chance it afforded her to escape this iceberg if it came down to that.

She came to an abrupt stop twenty feet from her car.

The man from this morning was back and he was leaning against her car!

CHAPTER THREE

Fortune Favors the Bold

Taking her in I said, "You look tired. Coffee or hot chocolate?" I asked, holding up each hand that held a cup in turn.

Blinking repetitively she stared at me for a moment before emotionally saying, "Get away from my car!"

"No." I said succinctly before adding, "Not before you answer the question."

Fury rose up into her face and I saw her fight an inner war.

I remained still as I evaluated the odds of her drawing her gun and shooting me as a distinct possibility.

In fact, I put the odds around 17%.

Cajolingly I said, "Simmer down and accept some southern hospitality. I'm not an owner of slaves and you're no slave yourself, except perhaps to the wealth of bitterness I see you have stored up inside of you."

She blinked and then accused sharply, "What do you think you know about me?"

"A great deal actually, especially as you continue to glare daggers into me with those gorgeous eyes of yours, baby girl. Now it's getting chilly. Which will it be?" I said, shaking both cups.

Gradually then she moved closer and took the hot chocolate out of my hand. I didn't miss how careful she was not to touch my hand in the process.

"Ahhh, I see you have a sweet tooth. That's okay by me, because as of late, I find myself partial to coffee. Hot and black with no sugar added."

It took her a moment to get it and when she did she said a very un-ladylike thing to me and it was a last moment thing that the cup of hot chocolate wasn't chucked at me.

Breathing hard, she looked away and I took the moment to enjoy the vision of her.

Glancing back, she said with hard fought reserve, "Please move away from my car."

"Yes, ma'am." I said and smoothly stepped away, but in the process got closer to her.

She jumped back.

"Relax Honey, I promise I don't bite hard. That said, God surely did create parts of you to be nibbled upon."

"Have you no shame?" She yelled at me.

"When it comes to being honest, no, ma'am, I don't."

She hurriedly stepped around me and got into the car.

"Enjoy the hot chocolate." I said, as with a screech of tires she peeled out of the parking lot.

I stood there watching her car go out of sight before taking a sip of my coffee. It wasn't all that satisfying, as I in truth, liked my coffee with a bit more sugar.

If the girl could stroke a stray cat, as she had with a smile, then she could no doubt do the same for me one day. She just needed to be tamed to my touch.

I heard him approach, but I didn't turn to acknowledge the presence of the sheriff.

He spoke, "I see ya's taken a liking to the new darky ain't ya Zeke. Wouldn't get too fond of her now if I was you."

I let my gaze slide over to land upon him and making direct eye contact I said, "Not one hair of her head had better be harmed or there will be hell to pay. Comprende?"

Blinking the sheriff nodded and I left him there. I had no use for men like him.

He'd taken my threat seriously, but rat that he was, I knew at some point that he would need to have a reminder.

~~~~~~~~~~

The Next Evening – Mandy's Perspective

Mandy made her way towards the parking lot cautiously. She hadn't seen him or his truck around town all day, but it paid to be cautious.

Approaching her car she came to a dead stop just short of it. Something was sitting on top of her cruiser.

It was small though, and approaching closer she saw that it was a coffee cup, only she knew that it would have hot chocolate inside of it instead.

Pursing her full lips together she reached up and picked the cup up. It was still warm.

With her other hand, she picked up the note that had been underneath it and in the evening gloom read it aloud, *"Dear Mandy, at times I speak my mind too much, even so as to make my own mother ashamed of me. I came off crudely yesterday. I apologize. Please accept the hot chocolate as a token of my...... um..... not sure what."*

The corner of Mandy's mouth lifted in a smile that she couldn't hold back.

She glanced down and read the **P.S.** *"I feel I need to clarify something. Coffee has never tasted as good as you look. Sincerely meant, Zeke Daniels."*

Shaking her head Mandy looked away from the note.

The man couldn't help himself.

He wouldn't be happy until he had her stripped naked and accepting his white man's cock. It was most likely a big one too.

She shook her head to clear her mind of the last thought.
~~~~~~~~~~

Where had it come from anyway?

All he wanted was to get a taste of something exotic.

Even as that may be the case he was certainly more charming than most in the way that he was going about trying to get it, or better put, her.

She sipped from the cup, it was very good hot chocolate.

Tucking the note into her pocket, she got into the car and screamed.

He caught the cup before its contents could go spilling across the car. Deftly he handed it back out to her with not a drop spilled from it.

Breathing heavy after what felt like the fright of her life she stared at him incredulous.

Why wasn't she fleeing the car or pulling her gun?

Her foggy senses came to a steady realization that shook her to her core. The reason she did neither was because she knew somehow that this man would never hurt her.

That realization made her all of a sudden all the more afraid. She simply didn't know what to do.

Swallowing, she glanced forward and asked, "Why are you stalking me?"

"I'd give you an answer, but you wouldn't like it."

Mandy glanced at him.

Nodding her head, she said, "Well, at least you're honest. Now if you think I'm going to leave this parking lot with you in my car you've got another thing coming."

"Actually, I was wondering if you could drop me off at my mountain? You see my truck is in the shop getting worked on."

Mandy gave him a long look and then asked, "Your mountain?"

"Yeah, I own one outside of town about two clicks from here."

Sudden awareness made her say, "You were in the military?"

His open face of charm closed off a little, but he did incline his head in a nod of affirmation.

"Let me get this straight, you want me to drive you out to your place, a secluded place mind you, after nearly scaring me to death and admitting in no uncertain terms that you are indeed stalking me?"

"That's right."

Shaking her head, she stated with emphasis, "You sure have a lot of ball to ask me to do something like this."

He smiled winningly and stated, "Two of them actually."

Her face flushing hot with embarrassment Mandy turned on the car and started driving.

Right now the best way to get rid of this man was to take him to where he wanted to be taken to.

As she drove she expected him to talk, but surprisingly he remained silent. Along the drive she kept glancing at him warily, but his gaze remained on the road ahead.

He pointed to an off-road and said, "You can stop here. I'll walk the rest of the way."

Dutifully she pulled over. His door opened and glancing over she watched him get out.

He walked around the front of the cruiser and again she was reminded of the fact that he was a very well put together man. He didn't move like a big man at all.

He had a cat like grace about his movements that told her that despite her defensive training, he'd likely have her laid out flat in a heartbeat. It was unnerving to have to admit that to herself.

He came up to her window and tapped it with a knuckle that bore the evidence of previous scar tissue. Not sure why she did it she lowered the window anyway.

He took a long moment of staring at her before he began to speak, "I was in the military. I had a lot of friends during my time in that I saw get hurt and some of them died. Thing was it didn't matter whatever creed or ethnicity that they were in life, because when they were cut they all bled red. Do you get what I'm trying to say?"

Shakily Mandy breathed out, "I think so."

Nodding, he said, "You're right to be on your guard around here, but you have absolutely nothing to fear from me."

Straightening up, he said, "Thanks for the ride. And by the way I really like your smell. It says a lot about you. My senses are overly acute to put it mildly. I can barely stand to be around most people simply because of how they smell, but you are really fine, a little on the bitter end, but with a definite underlying aura of sweetness."

That was it. He was gone then and so help herself, Mandy wasn't able to take her eyes off of him and kept staring long after he had disappeared into the darkness.

She pitied the creature that should seek to tangle with him in the dark.

Gathering herself, she turned the cruiser around. It was going to be a long six months.

CHAPTER FOUR

A Rebel like Him

One Month Later – Mandy's Perspective

Things had been quiet until today.

Sirens roaring Mandy did her best to follow the directions being flashed at her by her inboard navigation.

A report had come in from the locality of an alleged drug house of a woman in severe condition. It was unclear if the condition was drug-induced or from physical battery of some kind.

Paramedics were on the way, but they had to come from one county over. She was going to be the first responder.

Nervousness threatened to steal whatever calm she could manifest so she prayed for strength and the ability to deal with the situation that she found.

She made the last turn and the dump of a house trailer, which had meth lab written all over it came into sight.

In the same instance that she saw the trailer she saw something else that made her heart sink below the floor board of the car.

Zeke's truck was parked outside the trailer.

Cold fury chilled through her veins, until it turned her heart to ice. All the charm and sweet niceties that he'd been about over the last month went out the door in a flash.

Slamming the car into park she raced into the house's open doorway gun in hand. She stopped in horror at the sight of a naked woman covered in blood caused from a bad head wound lying on the floor.

The woman wasn't alone. Zeke was on his knees before her with blood all over his hands.

The woman herself was of mixed ethnicity. She was actually the first she had seen in Smithville other than herself and the color of blood on a pair of white man's hands made something inside of her snap.

"Get away from her!"

Zeke looked up. Consternation swept across his already worried face.

Oh, he better be worried!

Mandy's boot connected with his shoulder and he fell backward.

With a roar he was back on his feet and knowing she couldn't match him in a fight, she drew her stun gun and fired it from the hip. It was the only mercy he would get from her as more than anything else she wanted to fill him full of lead.

He jerked and fought far longer against the current than most, but in the end he passed out cold on the floor just as the ambulance roared up outside. The paramedics raced in and Mandy got out of their way.

They had the girl out and on the way by the time that Zeke started to stir.

She'd already handcuffed him and kicking him in the ribs hard she said, "Get up scum!"

He did get up. His mouth was strangely silent for once.

In fact, he didn't say one word to her all the way back to town.

No one was in the office and so she put him directly into a jail cell. She didn't undo the handcuffs, but turning the key in the cell door she walked away.

Behind bars was where a lying rebel like him deserved to be.

This was the reason why she had fought so hard to get through the Academy.

It felt good right now. She was making progress on a lengthy past of heaped up misdeeds by white trash such as the one behind her, who she hoped would rot away in jail for what he'd done to a woman of color.

All that said she still had a hollow feeling inside that she couldn't quite explain.

It didn't matter anyway, so she buried it.

~~~~~~~~~

Two Hours Later – Mandy's Perspective

The sheriff came into the office in a rush.

Mandy stood up and was about to speak, when the sheriff burst out with, "You stun gunned Zeke Daniels and arrested him?"

"Yes, Sir. He...."

"What on earth for ya dunce! Didn't you hear over the radio that the attacker fled the scene?"

Unease swept through Mandy, the radio had been squawking, but she'd been too hyped up to really pay attention to it.

Then the Sheriff brought all of it home to rest and she felt sick to the pit of her stomach as he said, "She's his half-sister for pity's sake you numbskull newbie!"

Feeling on the verge of throwing up, she whispered, "His half-sister?"

"Oh, don't worry about that halfbreed whore, she's stabilized for the moment, but you!!! I'm gonna see that you never work another day as a cop in your life! His sister already named who it was and it's a drug running bastard from the big city blacker than you two darky sisters put together! Now get your butt into that jail block and get him out of there!"

Mandy moved away from her desk and did just that.

It felt like she was walking in a dream, only this one was a nightmare and suddenly her life had come to an end.
~~~~~~~~~

The key slid into the lock and numbly she felt it turn. Grasping the door she pulled it open and backed away.

She could not bring her eyes to leave the floor.

"She's stable and conscious Zeke. Hospital says it's just a mild concussion. Don't worry about this piece of worthless trash here. I'll have her in this very cell for assault and battery once you make a statement."

"That won't be necessary Sheriff, as I'm not filing any charges."

"Darn tooting the hell you are! Why I….."

"Shut up and drive me to the hospital!" Zeke said in a tone that wasn't loud so much as it held an authority that was a scream all on its own.

The sheriff shut up.

Both men were gone seconds later and Mandy was left alone.

Tears began to slide down her face and her whole body jerked on a deep sob.

Another sob followed and then they just kept coming one after the other.

Slowly she sank to the floor.

She'd almost killed an innocent man, a man who had been trying to save his own sister.

A man who hadn't even exacted revenge on her despite how much she so richly deserved it.

Crying out brokenly Mandy pleaded in sorrow, "Oh God, what have I allowed myself to become? Oh Jesus, I'm sorry! I'm sorry! Oh God, forgive me!"

She continued crying, but felt no peace.

CHAPTER FIVE

His Mountain

One Day Later – Mandy's Perspective

It was Saturday. The whole day had gone by somehow and now it was dark outside.

She still had her job thanks to Zeke. If the sheriff had disliked her before now he absolutely hated her.

It didn't matter really, because for the most part she no longer had any self-respect.

None.

Zero.

Life was very gray right now.

The future...... what was her future?

A slight disturbance nearby sparked her attention. It was Ma Brown the owner of the café.

Suddenly she realized just how late it was.

Mandy stood up abruptly, "I'm sorry! You should have been closed up by now. I'll be on my way."

Making to go she stopped as the old woman's fingers closed about her wrist. Mandy met the old woman's kindly gaze and felt undone inside by the love she saw in the old woman's eyes.

White or not this woman genuinely cared for her.

Softly Ma Brown said, "Honey, there's no rush. Come here."

Out of any control to stop from doing so Mandy stepped into the old woman's arms and hugged her even as she was hugged in return.

Crying, she pressed her face into the old woman's shoulder even as Ma rubbed her back and made the comforting noises only a woman who had raised children of her own could fully understand.

Emotional outburst temporarily assuaged Mandy pulled back, "Sorry, I'm getting you all wet."

Ma chuckled, "Wouldn't be the first time and I dare say nor the last. Sit down Honey and I'll get us some hot chocolate."

Mandy sat down.

Still teary the tears began to flow harder again as she debated on what hot chocolate connotated a memory of.

A cup was set down in front of her and she stared at it for a long moment, before lifting misery ridden eyes to Ma sitting across from her at the small table. Ma reached her hand out and Mandy laid her black one into the aged white grasp of a woman that could care less about whether some people came in the color purple or any other color for that matter.

For Ma people were people and the only distinction was whether they were good or bad.

Meeting Mandy's gaze Ma said, "You know he really cares a lot for you right?"

Mandy did know and nodded her head, even as she bit her lip to keep from sobbing.

"Breath, Honey."

Mandy sucked in a deep breath.

Looking down, she whispered, "I've never had a man court me like he has. He…. he made me feel special."

Ma nodded her head.

Mandy looked up at her and brokenly she whispered, "I didn't know what I had! I let my past bitterness write my future and now the future I didn't even know that I wanted is gone! I almost killed him! It was his sister!"

Ma smiled bittersweetly, "Past issues and bitterness have a way of blinding us at times don't they. They make us do irrational things and they cause a lot of harm to others, but mostly to ourselves. I know you're a woman of faith Mandy. Have you asked for forgiveness?"

"Yes, but I don't feel any."

"That's because you want to punish yourself too much. We're our own worst enemies sometimes. Now let's evaluate the situation. Zeke is fine, the half-sister is stable, and you even have your career left to you. Seems to me someone upstairs went to a very thorough degree to see that no lasting damage came out of a series of bad choices on your part. This is a wake-up call, Mandy."

"I know."

"I'm not the enemy, Mandy."

"I know."

There was silence for a long moment as Ma rubbed Mandy's hand consolingly.

Ma spoke, "I have never seen that man smitten with a girl like he is with you."

Mandy's head only hung lower.

"Do you know what tomorrow is?"

"Sunday." Mandy said, looking up.

"Right! I will be by to pick you up at ten o'clock sharp. No protesting now, because I won't accept no for an answer. You're just going to have to humor an old woman and that's that."

"Where are we going?"

"To the mountain."

Mandy's eyes widened and she exclaimed, "His mountain?"

"Yep."

"Why?"

"Because that's where I go most Sundays. You might not believe it, but your man is a great preacher."

"Preacher? Zeke!" Mandy exclaimed.

"I know he's a bit rough and well, a bit forward with his manner of speaking at times, but let me tell you what, the boy can preach the Word of God and say what needs saying. Some Sundays half the town goes out to his place. As for the other half that don't go they can get up and leave town for all I care."

"How…. why?" Mandy stuttered out with still in complete wonderment of the thought of Zeke being a preacher.

"Why does he preach you mean? He saw a need. He invited people to come pray on issues the community was facing and ever since then it has grown, until now when it is just a regular occurrence to go there during fair weather and attend the local church for an evening service later in the day. Even the pastor of the local church goes out to Zeke's place." Ma stopped talking and silence dragged for a long moment as Mandy stared at her at a complete loss for words.

Ma chuckled and said, "In case you didn't know it Mandy, Zeke is a very special person. Someone else in this room is too. Together, both of you are going to make a very special couple. In fact, you're going to be just what this town needs."

"I….."

Ma waved her hand and said, "Don't say a word. Take your hot chocolate with you and go to bed. I will see you in the morning."

Before Mandy knew it, she was being hustled out the door and the lights in the café went dark.

Mandy stood still in the gathering shadows outside the café.

Slowly she took a sip of her drink and then did as ordered.

The mood of the day was much different now, much more hopeful.

And to some degree more redeemed feeling.

CHAPTER SIX

Almost Heaven

I liked the view. I'd always found this bare rocky promontory a good place to pray and the idea had sparked the thought that maybe others would too.

Before long a hundred people or more were showing up on Sunday mornings if the weather was fit, but this morning the only view I was taking in was the dress wearing vision sitting next to Ma Brown, who in turn looked like the cat that had swallowed the canary.

There was an undercurrent going on and I felt the weight of multiple pairs of eyes switching back and forth from me to Mandy as if we were a spectator sporting event.

My gaze met Mandy's and I saw everything in her face that I was hoping I would. That said she looked so bound up inside that even breathing looked like it was hard.

She was very sorry and yet I had known that ever since the time in the jail when she had let me go.

In addition to being sorry I could also tell it was taking every ounce of courage for her to be here.

For her this was an entirely new leaf she was turning over.

I smiled warmly at her and then taking in everybody else I said, "Let's talk about forgiveness this morning."

Quite a few smiles bloomed to life and almost everyone glanced at Mandy.

She blushed, but she bore the scrutiny well and the gradual realization that she was here for me became even more real.

I spoke out of a higher spirit than I had felt for the last two days, even as I thanked God for bringing her here.

The girl didn't know it yet, but she was staying for lunch.

~~~~~~~~~

She watched me intently during the whole talk and when things were coming to a close and I had a chance I mouthed to her, "*Stay*."

I wasn't sure she would listen and do it, but to my joy she did.

I'm not sure that she had all that much of a choice because Ma Brown got up and left almost immediately and to my surprise everyone else left hurriedly too.

How considerate of them.

Walking over across the rocky terrain I sat down on the edge of the same boulder that Mandy was sitting on. "Next time you should bring a cushion. These rocks get pretty hard after a while."

Mandy was quiet and then I watched as slow tears began to make their way down across the beautiful skin of her cheeks.

Finally, looking at me she worked hard to say, "I…. it's not enough, but…. I'm sorry."

I nodded my head and said, "Already forgiven."

She closed her eyes and glanced away.

Whispering she said, "I thought I was a better person than you and I'm not even close. How much else have I been blind too?"

I wanted to speak, but I felt pressure to remain silent within my spirit and so I did. She did something, then that was completely unexpected.

Reaching into her purse she pulled out of all things a stun gun. She laid it down on the boulder beside me.

"You can use it on me. I owe you far more, but if it helps you feel better then go ahead."

Wrinkling my brow I picked it up and handed it back to her, "It would make me feel worse to see you in pain, not better. Didn't you
~~~~~~~~~

listen to the talk earlier? Forgiveness means exactly that. There's nothing left you have to repay. It's done."

Several big tears rolled down her cheek and as Mandy took the stun gun back, she whispered, "Thank you." Then added, "I know what you said is true. It's just that you were innocent and I nearly killed you and then I drug you away from your sister when she needed you most. Heck, I even kicked you in the ribs. Did I break something?"

"Nah, I've had worse."

"I just feel like I shouldn't be let off so easy. I even still have my job thanks to you."

"So what you're saying is that if you received punishment of some kind you would feel better and be able to move on?"

She looked away, "I guess so, I don't know."

"Well, as the offended party, it's my right to pass judgment, yes, definitely I deem it to be so. Okay then, it's final I've settled on a punishment worthy of your crime."

I tried to maintain a serious expression, but I must have given myself away somehow as I saw her full lips part in a smile.

Pursing them back together, she faced me and asked, "Oh really, so what is my sentence?"

"I sentence you to having to be designated as my official girlfriend."

She didn't run and surprisingly didn't even protest.

Looking down at her folded together hands, she said, "When I was a little girl I made myself a promise never to be with a white man."

I stayed silent.

She glanced up at me then and with a shaky release of breath she said, "I guess some promises are better left to be broken than kept. I don't want to be the woman that almost pulled the trigger on an unarmed innocent man or the one that held the trigger of a stun gun eight seconds longer than you're ever supposed to."

I looked away and nodded my head as I said wryly, "Yeah, that was quite a jolt. But like I said I've had worse."

I looked back to her quickly as I felt her hand hesitatingly close over my sun bronzed one.

Gazing at the joining of her hand with mine for a moment I then let my eyes rise to hers.

Her gaze was open and I saw tenderness reflected in the deep depths of her eyes as she looked at me.

She was crying again, and I didn't hesitate.

I reached for her and pulled her away from the boulder only to transfer her to sit on my opposing thigh. She wasn't a small woman, but then I wasn't small either and as she sat I couldn't help but notice how perfectly in proportion we were to each other.

I could feel her whole body shaking and reaching up a hand I let it slide in to warmly cup her soft cheek and direct her to look at me.

She did so with reluctance.

Softly I said, "Hey beautiful, I'm going to kiss you now. Don't run away, okay?"

I felt her shake even harder, but she stayed put as my lips met hers even as we stared into each other's eyes.

The taste of her was sweet and unable to help myself I aggressively discovered her lips and then her mouth as if I was a kid gone wild in a candy shop.

She turned into me and one hand came to rest against my neck, and that is when I felt her begin to kiss me back. It was tentative on her part and yet utterly feminine and also quite virginal.

I opened my eyes only to see hers shut as she lost herself in what I had a feeling was her first kiss ever. I hadn't expected this and somehow it only made her sweeter still.

In need for air she broke her lips away from mine breathing hard.

I took the opportunity presented and claimed her neck with my lips and then the underside of her sleek jaw.

She moaned and lifting both hands she caught my face and brought it away.

Staring deeply into my eyes, she pleaded, "Tell me your intentions are honest! Tell me I'm not just a novelty lay for you!"

Reaching up I claimed both of her wrists and pressed a kiss into each of her palms.

Meeting her gaze, I said, "I promise that everything I share with you is from the heart."

She surrendered then and I reclaimed her lips for a very long time. I desired this girl beyond any I'd ever had before her.

I sensed that she was like clay in my hands that I could do absolutely anything with that I wanted to at the moment. As heady of a temptation as that was I wanted her for my wife even more.

Sensing the limit of my better judgment had been reached I left off kissing her.

Her lips tried to follow mine and chuckling I said, "Let's go for a walk."

I brought her up to her feet all the while ignoring the posturing and sexual languor her body was exhibiting that clearly said '*Take me now!*'

I would. Oh, I surely would, but not today.

Her hand in mine I walked along the scenic mountain trail of my home.

Her scent was a heady aroma that endlessly sparked desire and I bathed my senses in it even as I catalogued every new thing I was learning about her.

Being discreet wasn't my way and boldly I said as I squeezed her hand, "You've never had sex before."

It was fascinating to see how a black girl could blush. She didn't deny the truth, though.

"You know I want you for more than just your hot body."

"Do you?" She asked uncertainly.

"Yes, I do."

"What do you want?"

"I want to not be lonely anymore. I want someone, in fact, just you, to talk to. Someone, you, whom I can confide all my secrets and desires to. Someone I know I can trust and in turn be trusted by and that someone is you. I'm a good cook, but a lousy housekeeper. I can make you smile, but I can frustrate you to your last straw too. In short I plain want to be with you. I want to hear you breathe as you sleep at night. I want to see your face when you wake up in the morning."

We had stopped walking and now stared at each other.

"I want to say I love you and hear you say it to me in return. Better yet, I want to see it as you make my life special with your efforts to witness of your love. I want to enjoy and unlock all the secrets of your body. I want to stroke you to passion's height and hear you scream and beg for more. Most of all I want to feel and cherish how wonderful it will be to be inside of you and know that through our joining that a family can be made so that what I want us to share together can not just be for us, but for however many blessed souls God permits to be seeded into and born forth from your womb. Mandy, I don't want a day or even just a month with you. I want you to stay with me and be my wife for the rest of your life." I stopped talking.

Her reaction wasn't what I was expecting at all.

In fact, I really didn't know what to expect from having bared my heart of all I felt in regards to her and what I wanted to share together with her.

Before my eyes she literally dissolved into a bucket of tears with sobs so violent it looked like they hurt her.

"Honey? I......"

The rest was unsaid, as she suddenly lunged forward and pressed her face in against my neck to sob, "Oh God, I want that too! I never dreamed He'd give me my dream and to think I almost killed it with my own hand!"

Fully relaxed now I nuzzled my face into her hair even as I stroked her back and patted it and said, "You really need to move on from what almost happened and enjoy what God is doing in the present."

"I know. And I am!" Her lips found mine then and it was she who was the aggressor.

One of her toned thighs rubbed against the outside of my hip in an instinctual caress that was as old as Eve. Reaching down with both my hands, I had the cherished feeling of sliding my hands onto her butt for the first time.

The halves of her bottom nestled into the palms of my hands with a perfect abundance and groaning with the desire to strip her naked and see what my hands held I lifted her up and her thighs immediately locked together around my waist even as her passion swollen lips mashed into mine with a welcome I had only thought possible in my dreams.

Her full breasts softly mashed into my chest only to conform to the harder planes of my muscles.

Pulling my head back I saw a woman lost in the desire to both please and feel pleasure.

Husky voiced I said, "A first date shouldn't go as far as we both want it to right now."

Sighing she nodded and with reluctance her thighs parted away from their clasp of me and with even more reluctance I let my hands slide away from their grip of her bottom as I set her back down on the ground.

"Well, as punishments go, how did that feel."

She giggled and I fell in love with the sound of it. She didn't move away but stayed cozied up against me.

"It felt wonderful. Thank you, Zeke."

"For what?"

"For being a gentleman. I thought you were a rebel, but I was wrong. I discovered something yesterday, when I thought I had lost every chance of being around you ever again. I...... I love you.

"Smiling, I said, "I know."

Looking at me in wonder she asked, "What made you pursue me?"

"Well to be honest the sight of your butt as you were bent over stroking the neck of that kitten alerted me across every nerve to the fact that I wanted you, but it was the sight of your smile that told me you were what I've been waiting for and hoping that God would bring me."

Not offended in the least at my frankness she smiled and taking my hand we then walked back the way we had come.

I drove her home and spent another hour kissing her at the door of her apartment.

Tearing myself away I went home only to not sleep the rest of that night. Before the sun had risen I was in town and parked outside her apartment with coffee I had made at home.

All night I had wondered at just how abbreviated of a courtship, she would put up with. The most pressing question being, was she okay if we got married today?

I knocked on her door, anxious to see her, but abruptly stilled inside as what should've been a locked door fell open inwardly several inches with a rusty creak.

My old life of being always a second away from sudden-death claimed me once more even as the coffee cup fell to shatter on the floor.

I slammed the door back so hard the handle sank into the drywall and in that same instant I confirmed that the room was empty and worst of all I knew the most likely reason for it.

They had come for her.

The '*they*' being the cowardly, sniveling dogs that every society in one form or another was cursed with. The proverbial, '*them*' in this case, though had made a terrible mistake.

They should have never stolen something away from a man, who wouldn't stop at anything to reclaim it, no matter what the cost might be.

CHAPTER SEVEN

The Dark Side of Man

Mandy flexed her fingers. The cuffs were tight.

They belonged to the Sheriff and even though they all wore hats to make themselves look like ghosts, it was easy to tell who was who.

She'd been so close to happiness, and now one day away from the heaven of yesterday she was fast approaching the dark of another night that would see her doom if something positive didn't happen soon.

The only thing that could happen positively though, was if Zeke came for her and intrinsically she knew that he would.

Her mouth tasted of blood from where her split lip still bled. The Sheriff had backhanded her earlier, while another of his accomplices had held her hands behind her back.

The puffed up little curr!

She longed to be free of the cuffs binding her for just three seconds, so she could make a eunuch out of the little rat hiding behind a badge and a pillow case.

There were twenty or so of them, which really was a miniscule amount when upon arrival in town she through her own prejudice would have classified every person in town as someone who would've attended a gathering such as this.

She had been wrong. She had been wrong about a great many things.

She was right about something though. Her man, he had come for her.

The torches that lit up the grove of trees where a rope hung down from an oak branch became the only noise to be heard as with a hushed calm all the shotguns and pistols of nervous cowardly men trained upon a man whose boots they weren't noble enough to fill in three lifetimes.

Mandy watched Zeke draw close and then pass by her.

What was he doing?

At least one of these cowards would shoot him!

Every eye was drawn to him as he came to a stop beside the noose hanging down from the oak branch. Stooping down, he picked up a lit piece of wood from a nearby fire that she'd gotten the impression would be used to burn her corpse in after they had hung her or perhaps she had it in reverse.

It was anybody's guess now, as Zeke was putting a peculiar slant to the night.

With the makeshift torch he set fire to the rope. It crackled into flame and as if mesmerized everyone watched the flames trace up the length of rope.

Mandy felt something behind her then.

The cuffs were gone!

Glancing back, she saw her fellow deputy and holding a finger to his lips, he gestured for her to follow him.

Quickly she scuttled away from the stake she had been bound to only too eager to be away, but at the same time anxious for the fate of her man.

She resisted against Bryant and glancing at her, she pointed to Zeke only to hear him whisper in return, "Trust me, he can take care of himself."

That may indeed be the case, but why not help?

Pulling to a stop, she looked back just in time to see the burning rope fall to the ground.

All eyes swiveled back to Zeke and then to something burning in his hands.

Mandy gasped in concert with all the hooded executioners, as she took in the sight of what were two lit sticks of dynamite in each of Zeke's palms whose short fuses were visibly fizzling away.

Shotguns were dropped and stumbled over as would be henchmen on the side of evil ducked for cover.

"Zeke!" Mandy cried out as the fuses burned low.

She made to run for him, but Bryant held her back. The fuses sputtered and then went out.

The sticks of dynamite were duds!

Slowly the hooded gathering glanced up from where they lay huddled on the ground.

Zeke spoke, "That's right; you were all scared of nothing. You know why? It's because you don't have anything for a soul to lend you courage. Every last one of you has been a cancer in this town for years. The right thing to do would be to string up every last one of you and then cast your bodies into a tar pit and set it ablaze. Unfortunately, though the current rule of law doesn't permit that kind of behavior no matter how well deserved it is in your cases and frankly none of you are worth going to prison over. So the town of Smithville is going to be content with the fact that every last one of you is leaving this night with nothing more than the costumes you have on and none of you are ever coming back. If you do, rest assured we'll find a place for you to eternally rest where no one will ever find you."

As Zeke had been speaking townspeople had been stepping forward out of the shadows with weapons of their own held at the ready. Quivering the group of gathered would be executioners took off running.

All but one cleared the light of the torches unmolested. The unfortunate one was the Sheriff and the enforcer was Zeke.

Zeke's hand flashed and the Sheriff cried out in pain only to find himself thrust down to his knees as blood flowed freely from his smashed lips and nose.

"Honey?" Zeke called out and trotting forward Mandy came up to him still dressed in the dress from yesterday.

Zeke held the Sheriff still who groaned and struggled at the sight of her before him.

Mandy didn't hesitate. Her leg drew back and she let the pointed dress shoe fly forward with all the force she could muster.

The pointed shoe sank deeply into the groin of the Sheriff, who abruptly sang out like a stuck pig in soprano.

Zeke jerked him up by his hair and shoved him forward after the others with a kick to his rear. "I warned you fleabag. Now go infest some other part of the world with your presence."

The Sheriff stumbled forward, moaning and clutching at his groin. He could still be heard for some time even after he was gone from sight.

~~~~~~~~~

Taking in Mandy I saw that she was physically well and despite the split lip, she was sporting she was smiling at me.

She stepped into my arms to nuzzle against me like the dream girl I'd always wanted to feel doing so, even as she was doing now.

"Well Sheriff, looks like Smithville is going to be a different place from here on out."

Mandy's head drew back, "What?"

"You heard me. We had a recent opening for the position, but you've just filled it. After all the position of Sheriff is a locally appointed one."

Mandy glanced at Bryant who, grinning shrugged his shoulders and said, "He is the Mayor after all."

Mandy's head whipped back around to me as she exclaimed, "The Mayor!"

Smiling, I pulled her hand up and slid something not nearly as precious as she was onto it.
~~~~~~~~~

Mandy went from her surprise of me being the town mayor, which pretty much amounted to nothing, to gazing at the facets of the diamond on her finger sparkling brightly by torchlight.

Her eyes huge she looked from me back to the ring and then back to me and I said, "Say, I do."

She started to speak, but holding up a finger I said, "But you have to mean for forever."

Without a pause, she said then, "I do vow to be yours forever, Zeke Daniels!"

"And I do to you the same, Honey. Now let's get the hell out of here!"

Ducking a shoulder down I flipped her over it and with an arm across the back of her legs, securing her safely in place I headed down out of this rough place that had seen far too many brutalities in the past.

Mandy was laughing, indeed so was the rest of Smithville for that matter.

Let them. It sounded good.

CHAPTER EIGHT

"I was right."

The sun was coming up when I pulled the truck to a stop at my house. I reached for her, but she ducked out of the truck laughing.

I got out of the truck. I was serious.

I wanted her. I needed her.

I'd almost lost her.

I didn't want to know what that felt like ever again, all the while though Mandy continued to back away from me.

A ready smile was on her face for me and it only caused the desire I had for her to increase. "Come here." I ordered, stepping out after her.

Laughing, she continued backing away and challengingly she asked, "Why?"

"Because I want you!"

"Then come and take me rebel boy!" She said and turned tail and ran.

Blinking, I ran after her only to see her come to a stop on the mountaintop vista that I had begun an outdoor church upon. As the sunlight lighted the land it cast her into sharp perspective as with a zip her dress came undone and fell to her ankles.

I stopped running and with a smiling glance back at me I watched her slide her bra off and let it fall to the ground.

Only her panties remained and feeling the thunder rush of my blood through my veins I walked toward her as she viewed the new sunrise barefoot and topless upon my mountain.

On the way to her I lost all my clothes, until free of them, I stepped up behind her and let my shaking hands discover the supple curves of a dream come true.

She pressed back against me as I slid my hands under her arms and palmed each of her soft warm breasts.

She glanced at me with that smile she'd given the cat and said huskily, "I thought you might like to take the rest off yourself."

I kissed her even as the turgidly erect shapes of her large nipples burned into my palms. My shaft lay wet and aching against her lower back.

Breaking off the kiss I sank down to my knees behind her dragging my hands down her luscious curves as I did so. My thumbs hooked into her panties and I pulled them down.

Presented with two twins of perfection I wetly kissed each one of them and then I turned her.

She looked down at me outlined by the sun behind her and said, "Make me yours."

"I will, but first I'm not done kissing you."

Directing her beautiful thigh to slide over my shoulder I helped her find her balance as she stood on just one foot. Ducking my head down I kissed the wet lips of her womanhood that I knew ached to feel my shaft part them.

She gasped and almost fell, but I held her steady, even as one of my wishes was fulfilled within the course of a minute.

As I wetly played with my tongue upon the jewel set at the core of her, she came with a loud cry and clutched at my head.

She would've fallen, but I brought her down safely to lay her down upon the bare stone of the mountain even as her gaze was filled with the sight of my cock as I shifted to kneel between her splayed apart thighs.

"I was right." She whispered.

"About what?" I asked, as I came down to be face-to-face with her even as the head of my cock nuzzled into the wet opening of her feminine place of welcome for no one else but me.

"You do have a big cock." She said shyly with a smile.

Smiling, I said, "Yes, I do, baby girl."

Her lips parted in a gasp as I slid into her sleek sheath. Meeting resistance I pressed against it and crying out she bit my shoulder.

"Easy little kitten. I've got a long way to go."

Her alarmed eyes came to mine as she released her bite, "You do!"

"Yes!" I said, kissing her even as I shoved the rest of my shaft all the way home into her wet tightness.

She cried out sharply into my mouth, but I didn't let her lips go free as I took her deeply over and over again until spurting out my seed within her depths I made her mine.

CHAPTER NINE

Something Forgotten

A year and a day later.

Mandy smiled as she came into the office. "Well is it done deputy?"

"Yes, ma'am he's in lockup."

"Good."

Going past him she said, "Don't disturb us as I will no doubt have to interrogate him and it might get ugly."

Bryant rolled his eyes and left the office. Closing the cellblock door Mandy walked up to the bars of the only occupied cell and taking a hold of them whispered thematically between them, "Well, are you sorry yet?"

Her indulgently lounging back against the wall husband smiled and with a stretch said, "About what?"

"About what? You still don't remember what yesterday was?"

He paused as if to think only to say, "No, I...... oh wait....... our anniversary."

"Oh, now it comes to him." Mandy accused playfully.

"Oh, it came to me before. That's why I bought this." At his words a necklace pendant fell from his hand to jerk and swing about on its golden chain.

Mandy gasped and reached for it.

Chuckling Zeke straightened and approached the bars.

"If you want it though you have to kiss me."

"Done! Coming here, Sugar."

~~~~~~~~~

Aggressively I kissed her as she pressed her face wantonly through the bars.

Groaning, she lost herself completely in the moment and with a smile I stepped away as something clicked shut.

Mandy blinked and then in startlement looked at her hands now cuffed around a bar.

"What? How did you…?"

I unlocked the cell door with the keys I had taken from her belt and the door of the cell swung wide open with a slight push.

"Why you rat!" She exclaimed with a fun-loving smile.

Smiling, I came up to her and said while holding the necklace in front of her face, "Now that is no way to be talking if you want this."

Her gaze turned playful and she asked, "Why, what should I do?"

"Just stay as you are only perhaps a little lower maybe."

"You can't be serious?" She whispered, as my fingers slipped around her and undid her belt.

"Oh, but I am. Now do as I say."

Dutifully she bent over at the waist as I slid her pants all the way down. I was greeted with the sight of a very becoming pair of boy shorts that soon went the way that her pants had.

Letting my hands slide over her bottom I stepped up behind her and undid my pants.

"What if Bryant comes in?" She whispered.

"He's on paid leave for the rest of today."

"You two planned this, didn't you?" She accused.

Chuckling the only answer I gave her was to slide my cock all the way into her already wet sheath.

Groaning gutturally she gripped the bars harder and moaned as I took her with domineering passion.
~~~~~~~~~

"I think they call this brutality of a police officer." She panted out with, only to then groan as I stroked into her deeply.

"Oh Darling, you have no idea. You're going to be chained up for the rest of the day."

Mandy glanced back at me and smiled only to push her rear back into me as I surged into her again. I heard her start to pant harder and then she came explosively.

Her orgasm complete I withdrew my shaft and knelt down behind her to feast upon the juices of her orgasm. She rose up on tiptoe as I licked wetly into the folds of her sheath and gasped out, "Oh God…. you didn't cum? Honey, oh oh…..ohhh, you're going to make me cum again!"

"That's the idea, Honey. Happy anniversary, Baby Girl." I don't think she heard the last part as she had already begun to scream as she became unglued in passion's grip completely unmindful of anyone hearing her.

I on the other hand heard every blessed note of her orgasm.

Standing back up I reburied myself into the heart of it even as I gazed down upon the beauty of her upturned rear that had been the first thing to catch my attention over a year ago.

"Thank you, God!" I said, meaning every word of it as I slid forward one last time and felt the peace of having my favorite person in all the world clamp tight all about me.

It was a sublime moment and I relished it to the full as my seed coursed into her explosively.

Breathing heavy we both stayed joined for a long moment.

Lifting her head, she glanced back at me with a smile and with a sigh of reluctance I pulled out of her.

She straightened up and leaning in against her we kissed each other. I undid one handcuff and she turned around into my embrace still kissing me.

Her eyes opened though when she heard the cuff reclose. Her full lips parted from mine as she glanced up at her wrist now refastened to a prison bar.

Her eyes full of seductive intrigue she glanced back at me once more as taking her other wrist I re-secured it to the bars on the other side of her head with a second pair of handcuffs.

"You weren't kidding about torturing me all day were you baby."

I smiled at her in answer, as I began unbuttoning her shirt and she immediately groaned and exclaimed, "Oh no, I know that look!"

"Oh?"

"Yes, you're going to make me cum again and then again and again. I won't be able to walk when you're done with me."

I chuckled richly even as I undid the front closure of her bra and let her beautiful black breasts spill free.

I pushed the bra and the undone shirt off to the sides of her breasts until they were framed by them and then I took the necklace I'd gotten for her and fastened it about her neck.

She glanced down and looked at the jeweled pendant resting just above the swell of her breasts, which my hands now held and lifted in to press around the sparkling jewels at the center of her chest.

"It's beautiful Honey, thank you." She said softly.

I kissed her.

Breaking the kiss off, I said, "No Honey, your what is beautiful, the necklace is just an addition to something already complete in perfection."

She smiled and then I ruined the tender moment by saying, "The necklace is like an artistic dribble of white icing on an already perfectly rich moist chocolate cake."

She laughed out loud and said, "Oh Honey, your terrible!"

I shrugged.

Her eyes grew serious then though, as she said, even as I stroked her large nipples with my thumbs, "But I love you!"

My mouth descended and I claimed one of her turgid nipples as my own and with a groan, she arched into me as much as her restraints would allow.

"Oh, why did you have to mention cake! Tell me you brought something to eat!"

I nodded, still latched onto her nipple and with her voice rich with promise she said, "Good because the baby is hungry."

Her nipple slid free from my lips and I gazed into her smiling eyes with shock.

"Happy anniversary present, Honey." She whispered.

I gazed down to the supple curve of her stomach, was it perhaps just a little rounder?

"Just think, Honey before the passage of too much more time you'll have some sweet white milk to go along with your moist rich chocolate cake."

What she had said had been funny, but I wasn't laughing.

Meeting her gaze, I whispered, "You're serious?"

She nodded and I immediately reached up to uncuff her, but she stopped me with an immediate protest of, "Don't you dare uncuff me mister! I want to be tortured and you promised it would take all day and I expect you to be a man of your word, Sir!"

Smiling, I kissed her and whispering against her lips I said, "You're amazing. You're sure you want to go on?"

"Make me scream rebel boy." She breathed back into my mouth, even as I felt myself become fully erect once more.

The woman had an amazing effect on me to say the least.

Reaching around her I palmed her beautiful bottom cheeks and lifted her up so that she hung suspended from her wrists with my hands her only support.

I felt her legs fasten about my waist and with a groan I slid back into the warm tight welcome of her even as her breasts rubbed erotically against my chest.

She and I locked lips in a kiss of sheer passion and love for each other as we celebrated the beginning occurrence of something we both immensely wanted. A family!

Life didn't get better than this moment and whispering I exclaimed, "Praise be to God!"

And as she lowered down deeply upon me she moaned, "Praise be to His mighty name! Oh Honey! I love you!"

She cried out with and came as she hung suspended upon my shaft.

Whispering against the sweaty skin of her neck I said the same even as I had the joy of listening to her moan her way through her orgasm.

I closed my eyes in simple relish of everything.

I was going to be a father.

Many things may be uncertain as to how good of a father I would be, but there was no doubt in my mind that no son or daughter could ask for more in the form of a mother and I would do my best to be a father in like degree of excellence.

It was a happy anniversary indeed!

THE END

Dear Reader,

A very short, but sweet book. I hope you enjoyed it. I find most of what I write is of a more serious nature, but hopefully more humorous works will be forthcoming in the future. A longer story that is also interracially charged, but not overly sweet would be, *The Huntsman*. It was the first story I wrote in this erotica adventure and it remains one of my favorites. A First Chapter Excerpt is on the next page. Enjoy!

Author's Corner

It would seem that the genre of Erotic Christian Fiction, which I have coined in terms of labeling what I have written, appears to be an entirely new avenue within the Fiction market. Many, who call themselves 'Christian' will not understand what I have taken upon myself to do and in general I expect reactions to what I've written to be hostile and that's okay. Why is that okay? The reason it is okay is because it is better to do what God says then stay hidden safely away within the mass of a group and only do what is perceived amongst the group as 'okay'. Truly the path to hell is paved with both the 'doctrines of man' and 'group think'. I write what I do, because I follow the leading of the Holy Spirit of God and nothing else. This avenue of Christian Erotic themed fiction is something He laid upon my heart to do and I chose to obey the calling and go wherever He wanted it to go. It is within my heart to be obedient to God always and to that end I have gone farther than I ever expected to be asked of me by my God in terms of witnessing to a lost and dying world, but even so, His will be done. If you have questions or comments, please feel free to direct them to me at the following email address: I don't always have answers, but I can pray for you and whatever I can't do – God can.

author-aedan-sayla@proton.me

Thanks for reading and please do leave a review!

The Huntsman

Chapter One

'Keep your head down, don't make eye contact, and above all don't do anything to look pretty.'

It was a daily litany of routine that I could barely stand anymore that was rivaled only by having to deal with how bad I smelled. Even the slop in the battered tin that my hands were wrapped around was almost beyond my ability to cope with in terms of smell or taste.

I wasn't entirely positive as to what it was that I was eating, but I had prayed over it and I hadn't been told by my God not to eat it so I ate it. Every cursed hack worthy bite of it each day I was blessed to even be fed.

I found my secret spot in the barracks where for a few moments each day I was fortunate to be out of sight of anyone. So far I had never been bothered here yet, but things could change.

So far today the record seemed to be in no threat of being broken.

Shivering, I dipped the battered spoon I kept hidden in a pocket into the runny broth and brought a bite up to my lips. It was at least warm, that much I could say about it, but otherwise having to daily consume it was like being in some proverbial dimension of hell. Being imprisoned, as I was, only made the aspect of being in hell more so in terms of appearance.

We were told though that the conditions outside were even worse. I'm not sure I believed the guards on that one entirely, but before being rounded up I had seen unspeakable things take place.

Things I would never have believed possible. Things that no matter as bad as this forced incarceration had been could not equal.

Still, I wanted to be free of this place, with its tall barbed wire walls and guards that would grab a hold of a boy or girl and haul them off to be raped by the whole squad on watch as a sort of payment for protection services.

No this place was hell and however bad as it had become on the outside in the last 2 ½ years I didn't care so long as I managed to at least die or live with dignity free from this daily torment of fear and expectation of pain.

The meager portion in the bowl was gone and I tucked it and the spoon away within my tattered cloak for tomorrow providing if whether we would be fed or not. As of late that wasn't always the case.

In fact the days of missed feedings were getting more and more frequent. The population of three thousand or so refugees only grew sicker and more malnourished because of the missed feedings.

I was the healthiest person I knew and yet in order to survive I had learned the wisdom of acting like I was sick and partially out of my mind in order to fit in with the rest of my inmates that I would barely classify as being human anymore.

Precious were the moments of the day when I could be alone and not having to pull off an act of half addled craziness. In these few blessed moments I often took the opportunity to speak to God, who in effect was my only surviving companion in this place of hell on earth.

He was the only one keeping me sane. Truly, without Him I would be as lost as the rest of these poor souls.

Closing my eyes, I clasped my hands together and said, "Lord, you got me through another day. I...... I'm grateful for the food I've been given."

A single tear streaked down my face, it was hard to choose to be real and not someone embittered by life's circumstances.

"I hope for something a lot better soon, but if that's not the plan then so be it. I'm still your girl. The people here are getting sicker and sicker and I fear where this is going. I've tried to speak to some of them of You, but nobody wants to listen. They're all so bitter and full of hate because of how they've been treated. Please keep me from becoming like them. I don't want to give up on my hope that this will change and get better, but oh God you've got to help me! I...... I'm falling...... I can't.....I......"

"Shhhh."

Immediately I hushed as the presence of my Creator washed over me and suddenly everything was made better, even though my surroundings remained the same.

I waited for God to speak to me either audibly or through the Spirit, but nothing came. I was on the verge of asking Him why He'd told me to be quiet when a disturbance at the door of the barracks caused me to hunch further back into my hiding spot.

Two guards came in and immediately my breathing sped up and yet I did my best to halt the rapid rise and fall of my chest. If I was found here by them it wouldn't matter how ugly I had made myself to appear as they were nothing but something worse than an animal in their treatment of those they supposedly guarded.

I had learned from new arrivals over the years that had been moved in from other FEMA camps that the conditions imposed were universal, if not worse in other places.

The government, it was clear, had fully intended for this type of treatment of its citizens and it seemed to me an act of cruelty that they hadn't just lined us up and shot us on the day we had arrived.

Maybe that was the point. Someone or something wanted us to suffer.

The guards came closer and with shock I saw that they weren't the usual motley crew. These guards were dressed rather a lot finer and their weapons and boots were shiny.

One spoke in perfect English, which was another shock as all the guards were foreigners formally of UN core divisions. The purpose of which was to ensure that they had no qualms in enforcing camp strictures because after all to them we were but foreigners being held within the bounds of our former country of America and thus nothing for them to be concerned about in terms of our welfare or peace of mind, as the stories of what had been done in this facility were unlikely to make their way home across the Atlantic Ocean.

The guards were some distance off from me, but I made out their words clearly, "This place should have been burned a year ago like the others. What a complete waste."

"Yes, why resources have been allocated this long is beyond me. It's going to end, though."

"Tomorrow?"

"Yes, I heard the order. Tomorrow we take them all out in the forest and shoot them."

"Shoot them? Why waste bullets on the likes of these scarecrows? Why not just crowd them into these flea holes and light them up?"

"It's the order is all I can say. Gives us an excuse to at least have a little fun tomorrow though doesn't it."

The other guard snorted, "I haven't seen one of these relics fit enough to run faster than a two legged cow with milk fever!"

Both men laughed and then left the barracks.

I stayed where I was staring wide-eyed into nothingness.

At long last I was getting my wish. I would be leaving Earth tomorrow by a means other than my own hand and I would see God and know no more pain.

I'd made it to an honorable end!

"No, Tamara." came the response from within the corridors of my soul.

My sudden found peace stealing away from me; I choked out with, "What?"

"Tomorrow you run child."

Shaking I looked about the barracks.

Run?

Run to where?

No further instruction came and my time away from the others was up.

I got up and made to rejoin the penned in citizenry of a once great nation now reduced to talking monsters in uniform and avokeless slaves at the mercy of cruelty's destiny.

Tomorrow I would run.

I had never been one for exercise and truly the last time I'd probably run was when I had been a child.

I definitely didn't weigh as much as I had before. Truth be told, my condition of being overweight going into this setup of forced incarceration might be one of the chief factors in why I was in as decent health as I was.

How ironic that was.

All the years I'd struggled with body image and weight that wouldn't come off was now a thing of the past and yet the means by which I had reached the present. In this world of the moment though no such vanity of times past mattered a hill of beans.

In fact, I could see the benefits of being a little fat now as opposed to the ultra-lean magazine imagery I'd always been striving for.

The question was did I possess the stamina to make a clean getaway tomorrow?

Whether I did or not that was what had been asked of me and so that would be what I would do.

I left the barracks and rejoined the act of fitting in with the rest and acting like I was half brain rotted.

All the rest of that day though an air of excitement tinged my perceptions of what was around me.

That night though it all changed. For hours I lay awake on my cot listening to the tormented dreams and discontented sighing of those I had been imprisoned with.

Tears streaked down my face as the abject truth of my failure to reach any of them with the saving Gospel, the truth of Jesus Christ, made its impact upon me especially hard. I had witnessed my faith, but I had never succeeded in converting anyone and right now the bitterness of my failure and being unprofitable for the Kingdom of God was crushing.

Tomorrow all of these people were going to die!

I felt like waking them up and speaking to them right now, but I knew it would do me no good. In a way I knew it wasn't my fault that no one had listened, but the knowledge of the future for these already tormented souls broke my heart even more than the loss of all my friends had.

Before everything had come to an end and America had ceased to exist as a nation I had been part of a traveling Gospel choir. We had been on tour and had just left Pittsburgh when the lights had gone out and the old church bus had come to a rolling stop.

In the weeks that followed we had scavenged for food and fought to protect each other as best as we could. That said, the utter depravity of humanity unchained and given over to abject paranoia had been staggering.

Desperate people did desperate things.

The men of the group eventually left the older women that couldn't keep up and those younger ones like me who wouldn't leave anyone behind. Things had gone from bad to worse without any men to help us and one night we were attacked by people so hungry it had driven them over the edge enough so that they crossed every frontier of saneness in order to feed upon their own kind.

I and three other girls had fled barely escaping with our lives. We were picked up soon after that and ferried by the government to this place.

At first it seemed like the reprieve of all reprieves, until after about six months when we all realized that we had arrived in a place of hell on earth.

It had been too much for the other three.

One girl got so weak because she refused to eat the food given to us that she became ill. In a matter of a month she was gone and her body thrown into the camp incinerator.

A month after that Ellie tried to make an escape through the barb wire, but got hung up in the wire. The guard towers had shown no mercy on her.

There were still nights I woke up in a sweat hearing the sounds of the gunshots and seeing the way her body had jerked about as the bullets landed. Worst of all they had not removed her body from the wire.

She had been the first to attempt an escape in the FEMA camp and it was made clear to one and all that she had better be the last. Her body was left to rot and day by day the crows picked and tore at the carcass until all that remained were shreds of cloth and a bone pile on the ground.

From that point onwards no one was left uncertain as to the reality of imprisonment we found ourselves all locked in.

About that time the American guards were shifted out and foreign speaking ones had been moved in. Most of them were Polish with the remainder coming from other Baltic nations.

With their arrival is when the rapes began.

Ellie's death in the attempt to escape affected me and Sissy, the last girl of the three, in an entirely different way. I remained content to bide my time for a better chance of escape, but Sissy gave up on the very idea of freedom being possible at all.

She had done the impossible in my opinion by turning her back on her faith one day and going to the guards. They had a standing offer of better accommodations and rations to any who would play the whore for them.

For a year Sissy had taken part in being used as a dishrag day and night as well as cleaning the guard compound, until in emptiness of spirit she'd taken her own life. Now I was all that was left of the South Carolina Gospel choir that had gone too far north and couldn't find its way back when darkness had fallen.

Tomorrow I would run.

Whether to my death or for continued existence I did not know, but I would do my best, even as I had done my best to survive to this day.

Tomorrow was all that I had left that I could lay claim to in life and it was firmly clenched in my mind.

I rested the rest of the night and then as the morning began I did nothing but breathe deeply. What I lacked in terms of energy and conditioning maybe could be offset by having extra oxygen to burn.

My father had been a pro athlete and after his career, he'd gone into sports medicine and I had picked up a lot of things just from hearing him speak. He had loved me, but always I could tell he was disappointed in the fact of me being overweight and not following in his footsteps like my younger brother and older sister had.

Now, however, I was lean and but I wasn't sick or emaciated like many of the others here with me were. However, I was still at a complete lack of vitamins, minerals and above all protein.

Couldn't be helped.

What I did have in bountiful supply was air. I had no limit to how much of it I could gulp down.

I fed myself on air and over the course of the morning I completely de-acidified my body and actually felt a lot better than I had in a long time.

Why hadn't I done this before?

I'd never had a reason to hope before was the answer to that one.

Knowing the likely fate of everyone else though continued to burden my soul. Just why was God giving me a heads up to run?

Didn't He care about anyone else here?

I felt immediate contrition at that thought. I knew better.

Softly came the voice of my Maker into my thoughts, **"None have listened, save one. None have obeyed My commands, save one. One is enough."**

~~~~~~~~~

Numbly I stood shivering in the cold with the rest of the compound. We had been rousted out of our barracks and had been pushed and shoved out into the muddy yard.
~~~~~~~~~

No explanation had been given and as it was we had been standing here for over two hours of which most of that time it had been lightly snowing.

It was colder feeling than usual today, because I had removed several layers of clothing that I had collected from the departed over the course of my long stay here. If I was going to run I needed to be free to move and not encumbered with extra baggage.

Also in these frigid conditions I needed to avoid all possibility of a chance of sweating. Better it was to be cold and dry than cold and wet, but right now as my teeth chattered I sorely missed my missing layers of clothes.

In a way it had felt like taking layers of armament off, an armament of filth anyway.

I perked up my head as a metal screeching sound was heard from the nearby forest. I'd heard the sound off and on over the last two hours, but this time the cause of the noise came into view.

It was a bulldozer. I swallowed.

There was a flurry of activity and the gates of the compound were thrown open. The coughing, shivering, massed throng that I was a part of looked from the open gates to an English speaking guard with a bullhorn.

He was one of the two from yesterday in the barracks.

"Attention everyone we are closing this camp. We're taking you to a safer place where you will be better cared for. Now please proceed in an orderly pace through the gates and down that track into the forest where you saw the dozer just come from. There will be food stations left along the way."

Like a pack of lemmings destined for a cliff face mass suicide the crowd of incarcerated citizenry eagerly took off in the direction they had been ordered to go. The combination of being half addled and the mention of food along with the idea of being anywhere but here took out any better sense of reasoning they might have otherwise formerly possessed.

I moved along with the pack, but purposefully I hung back towards the rear. I felt doing that offered me the best chance of cutting and running when the time came.

We were well into the grove of trees and I was on the verge of making my break, when an iron fisted grip seized about my upper arm and swung me around violently.

I gasped and gripped at the imprisoning hand, even as I took in the sight of the foreign guardsmen that had a hold of me. He was looking me up and down with interest and in that moment I realized that I looked far different than I usually did.

In despair, I heard him ask in broken English, "Why I don't see you before? All pretty ones gone, long time ago."

I said nothing and with a little shock suddenly realized that the column had moved on without me. I tugged upon the man's grip in order to rejoin the others, but he wouldn't let go.

The departing guards at the rear snickered and one called back in a Slavic language and made the motion of firing a pistol.

The one that held me grunted in affirmation and with despair I saw the column disappear around a bend and I was left alone with the guard, as the falling snow began to pick up in earnest. The guard's hold on me tugged abruptly and I found myself forced down to my knees at eye level with the man's belt buckle.

Breathing shallow I stayed where I was as the man undid his pants with his free hand and let them fall. I made to get up and move away, but he gripped a hand into my hair cruelly and held me in place.

With his other hand, he drew his revolver out and cocked back the trigger of it and brought the muzzle of the gun to press into the side of my head.

He laughed and with a cry of anguish I looked up at him, not believing that one could be so evil as this. He fully intended to blow my brains out the moment I finished sucking him off.

His grip on my hair only grew tighter. He shifted his engorging penis closer to my lips and with a grin said, "Open."

I'd rather die and to that end my teeth remained clamped shut even as he pushed his manhood that reeked of foulness against my lips.

He grunted angrily and pulled my hair so painfully that I was forced to cry out and he was just on the verge of capitalizing on my slipup, when screams rang out from the forest only to be suddenly drowned out by the rapid percussions of heavy gunfire.

The noise distracted the man and on desperate instinct I acted.

My hands came up and gripped at the hand that held the gun and with all my strength I moved his hand to position the gun against the man's own belly and with effort I managed to depress the man's finger on the trigger. The gun went off loudly.

The man cried out in consternation and his grip on my hair grew slack and I threw myself away from him. He collapsed down to sit cross-legged in the snow and stared on in horror at the blood pouring freely out of his body.

He began exclaiming expletives in his own language, as well as English, and I took my chance and ran for it. He turned the gun after me and started firing even as he screamed obscenities.

I dodged and a bullet slammed into a tree in front of me blowing bits of bark that stung my cheek painfully. I kept dodging and the gun finally clicked empty or maybe the man was dead, but I was alive!

I was also free!

I ran clumsily through the forest in a direction that took me away from both the compound and the scene of genocide further off to the right in the forest.

Dully it registered to me that I was headed north. I didn't much care where it was as long as it was away.

Gasping for breath I looked back. There was no visible sign of pursuit and best of all the snow was quickly making my earlier passage through the forest disappear.

As the miracle of the obscuring snow became realized for the true blessing that it was I looked heavenward and gasped out in praise, "Thank you, God!"

I was quite warm for the moment, but I needed to keep going. I moved forward still out of breath, but I didn't run this time.

I walked as quickly as I was able to, but as the adrenaline wore off over the course of an hour I feared that my time of freedom would soon be over.

The End of Chapter One Excerpt

*The rest of the story can be purchased at Amazon.com and other online eBook retailers **OR** you could check in with me via email and if you agree to leave an honest review a free review eBook copy of the book may be emailed to you.*

The choice is yours – in any regard I deeply appreciate the effort to support me in my work; however, it is given.

Sincerely,

Aedan